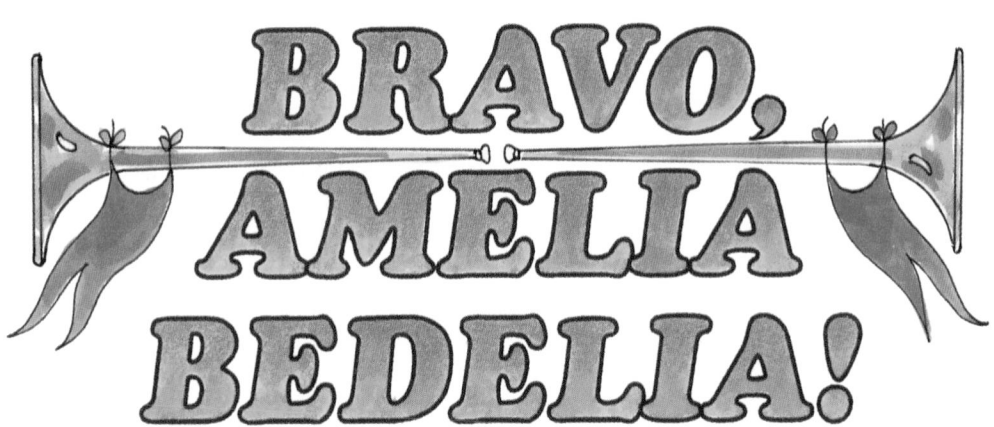

BRAVO, AMELIA BEDELIA!

By **Herman Parish**
Pictures by **Lynn Sweat**

SCHOLASTIC INC.
New York Toronto London Auckland Sydney

Watercolor paints and a black pen were used for the full-color art.
The text type is Kuenstler.

ISBN 0-590-12744-6

12 11 10 9 8 7 6 5 4 3 2 1   7 8 9/9 0 1 2/0

Printed in the U.S.A.   37

First Scholastic printing, September 1997

For Rosemary,
my lova
—H. P.

For Jennifer
and Sarah
—L. S.

It was the day of the school concert.

Mrs. Rogers was very upset.

"Where is Amelia Bedelia?

I sent her to the station two hours ago
to pick up our new conductor.

The orchestra is waiting to practice, and . . ."

"Yoo-hoo," said Amelia Bedelia.
"I'm back."

"Where is the conductor?"
 said Mrs. Rogers.
"I told you to pick up the conductor."
"I tried my best," said Amelia Bedelia.
"But he was too big for me to pick up."

A large man in a blue uniform
followed Amelia Bedelia into the gym.
"Oh, no!" said Mrs. Rogers.
"This man isn't the conductor!"
"He sure is," said Amelia Bedelia.
"Look at his uniform."

"I did not mean a *train* conductor,"
said Mrs. Rogers.

"I meant a *musical* conductor."

"He is very musical,"
said Amelia Bedelia.

"He whistled all the way over here."

Just then a man
in a nice black suit
jogged into the gym.
"I am sorry I am so late," he said.
"No one met me at the station."
"The *real* conductor," said Mrs. Rogers.
"Thank goodness you are here."

"Look, lady," said the other conductor,

"I like music, but I've got a train to catch."

"Catch a train!" said Amelia Bedelia.

"Be sure to use both hands.

Trains are heavy."

"Never mind," said Mrs. Rogers.

"I will drive him back to the station.

Amelia Bedelia, you help the other

conductor."

"Hurry back," said Amelia Bedelia.

"You do not want to miss the concert."

The conductor said hello to the students.
"Let's practice a few numbers," he said.
He waved his baton to start the music.
"One, two, and *three*!"

Amelia Bedelia kept on counting:

"Four, five, and *six*! Seven, eight, and . . ."

"Stop!" said the conductor.

"Did we practice enough numbers?"
asked Amelia Bedelia.

The children giggled.

"Don't count out loud,"
said the conductor.

"You can tap your toe, if you like."

Amelia Bedelia bent over to reach her toes.

Tap, tap, *tap!* Tap, tap, *tap!*

The children began to laugh.

TAP, TAP, *TAP!*

went the conductor's baton.

"Quiet, please. We have to practice."

He waved his baton.

The orchestra began to play.

Amelia Bedelia was enjoying the music

until a bee flew in.

"Shoo!" said Amelia Bedelia. "Go away!"

She tried to swat that bee.

She waved her arms around.

The conductor stopped the music.
"Miss Bedelia, *I* am the conductor.
Only *I* get to wave my arms around."

"Sorry," said Amelia Bedelia.
"There is a bee, see?"
"A-B-C?" asked the conductor.
"We are practicing music,
not the alphabet."

The orchestra started up again.
So did that bee.

"Excuse me," said Amelia Bedelia.

"May I borrow your pot lids?"

The boy laughed. "Sure. Here you go."

"Bye-bye, bee," said Amelia Bedelia.

Kee-RRRASH!

The music came to a halt.

"Miss Bedelia," shouted the conductor.

"We were playing a B-flat.
Would you call that B-flat?"

Amelia Bedelia looked at the bee.

"Absolutely," said Amelia Bedelia.

"A bee couldn't get any flatter."

"So you read notes," said the conductor.

"Only if they are addressed to me,"
said Amelia Bedelia.

"Do you play?" asked the conductor.

"I play every day," said Amelia Bedelia.

"Mr. Rogers says I'm an expert at fiddling."

The conductor handed her a violin.

"An expert fiddler," he said.

"Then you must play by ear."

"If you insist," said Amelia Bedelia.

She rubbed her ear across the strings.

"Ouch! Owie! Help!" cried Amelia
Bedelia.

A girl helped her untangle her hair.

"Expert fiddler indeed,"
said the conductor.
"Next time you should
use a bow."
"I'll use ribbons and barrettes, too,"
said Amelia Bedelia.
The conductor shook his head.
"You should try a different instrument."
"Which one?" asked Amelia Bedelia.
"Try the French horn,"
said the conductor.
"Or maybe another
wind instrument.
Or take up something
in the string section."

The audience began to come into the gym.

It was almost time for the concert.

Amelia Bedelia looked sad.

"Is there something I could play today?"

asked Amelia Bedelia.

"Only this," said the conductor.
"Anyone can play the triangle."
Amelia Bedelia was so excited.
She hit the triangle very hard.

"Play it lower!" said the conductor.

Amelia Bedelia sat down on the floor.

"I give up," said the conductor.

"Just hit the triangle *once* after
the drum roll and when you hear this."
He signaled to a boy to play the chimes.

"I'll get it," said Amelia Bedelia.
She ran for the nearest door.

"Come back here,"
said the conductor.
"Didn't you hear that doorbell?"
asked Amelia Bedelia.
"No one is at the door,"
said the conductor.
"When you hear those chimes,
you come in."

"That's easy," said Amelia Bedelia.
She opened the door and went out.

"Where are you going?" said the conductor.

"I have to go out before I can come in,"
 said Amelia Bedelia.

 She shut the door behind her.

"Good riddance!" said the conductor.

"I'll let her out after the concert is over."

Every seat in the gym was filled.

Mrs. Rogers got back just in time.

"*Now* where has Amelia Bedelia gone?"

said Mrs. Rogers.

She introduced the conductor

to the audience.

He waved his baton

and the concert began.

Amelia Bedelia heard the music start.

"I must listen for when to come in,"
she said to herself.

She looked around the storeroom.

"While I wait, maybe I can find
those instruments he told me about.

Where would I find a string section?"

She picked up a piece of rope.
"This is the only string I see,"
said Amelia Bedelia.
"I'll cut off a section later."

Amelia Bedelia looked some more.
"Ah-ha! Wind instruments.
Should I try a big one or a little one?"
She took the little wind instrument.

"Where would they put a French horn?"
said Amelia Bedelia.
She sat down to think.
"YEOW!" she cried.

She looked where she had sat.
"Lucky me—I found *two* horns.
They may not be French, but they'll do."

"Whoops! There's that doorbell again,"
said Amelia Bedelia. "I'm late!"
She flung open the storeroom door.
"Gangway! I'm coming in!"

The cord from the wind instrument
got tangled in her legs.
"Watch out!" said Amelia Bedelia.
She fell into the big bass drum.

The drum began to roll.

It rolled right at the conductor.

"Stop!" he yelled. "I said *STOP!*"

It stopped . . . after it ran into him.

The conductor was very mad.

"You ruined the concert, Amelia Bedelia!

What have you got to say for yourself?"

Amelia Bedelia didn't know what to say.

So she did what he had said to do.

She hit the triangle once.

All the students began to clap and cheer.

"What a cool concert," said a boy.

"I want to play in the orchestra," said a girl.

"Me, too!" said each and every one.

The conductor pulled Amelia Bedelia
out of the drum.

"Was that a good drum roll?"
asked Amelia Bedelia.

"You played it by ear,"
said the conductor.

"I used my whole body,"
said Amelia Bedelia.

Everyone was
standing up
and clapping.
The conductor
and Amelia Bedelia
took a bow.

"My gracious!" said Mrs. Rogers.

"Are you hurt, Amelia Bedelia?"

"I had fun," said Amelia Bedelia.

"But I'd rather fiddle around at home."

"*That* is music to my ears,"
  said the conductor.

The next day Amelia Bedelia made
a "thank you" note for the conductor.
She forgot to sign it.
But somehow the conductor knew
that it was from Amelia Bedelia.